Javier's Hummingbird

by Laura Driscoll
illustrated by Bob Ostrom

Kane Press
New York

For Rufus and Humma—L.D.

Acknowledgements: Special thanks to Meagan Branday Susi for providing the activities in the back of this book.

Library of Congress Cataloging-in-Publication Data

Names: Driscoll, Laura, author. | Ostrom, Bob, illustrator.
Title: Javier's hummingbird / by Laura Driscoll ; illustrated by Bob Ostrom.
Description: New York : Kane Press, 2018. | Series: Science solves it! |
    Summary: "Javier and Ana feed Rufus the hummingbird and explore solids,
    liquids, and gases as the nectar in their feeder freezes, melts, and
    evaporates"-- Provided by publisher. Includes activities.
Identifiers: LCCN 2017039189 (print) | LCCN 2017026124 (ebook) | ISBN
    9781635920086 (pdf) | ISBN 9781635920079 (pbk. : alk. paper)
Subjects: | CYAC: Hummingbirds--Fiction. | Matter--Properties--Fiction.
Classification: LCC PZ7.D79 (print) | LCC PZ7.D79 Jav 2018 (ebook) | DDC
    [E]--dc23
LC record available at https://lccn.loc.gov/2017039189

10 9 8 7 6 5 4 3 2 1

First published in the United States of America in 2018 by Kane Press, Inc.
Printed in China

Science Solves It! is a registered trademark of Kane Press, Inc.

Book Design: Michelle Martinez

Visit us online at **www.kanepress.com**

 Like us on Facebook
facebook.com/kanepress

 Follow us on Twitter
@KanePress

Abuelo and I are watering our flower seedlings.
"Can we move them outside yet?" I ask him.

My grandfather smiles. "Not until it's warmer,
Javier. Spring will be here soon!"

Just then, I see something flit past the window.
"Did you see that?" I ask.

"*¡Sí!*" Abuelo replies. "I did!" We stare out the window as a tiny bird zips into view. It hovers in the air. Then it rockets away.

"A hummingbird!" I call out.

"He's a little bit early," Abuelo says.
We see hummingbirds in our yard every
spring and summer. They fly up from the south
as the weather warms up. Then when autumn
arrives, they fly south again.

I love watching hummingbirds fly. They can change direction in a flash. Their wings beat so fast that they are a blur. They can even fly backward and upside down! No other bird can do that.

Abuelo says he thinks this one is a Rufous
hummingbird—a male.

"I'm going to call him Rufus," I say.

"Time to put the feeder out!" Abuelo says. He tells me that hummingbirds love red. It reminds them of the flowers where they get their food.

We fill the red feeder with a mixture of water and sugar. To hummingbirds, it tastes like flower nectar. *"¡Delicioso!"* says Abuelo.

Matter is anything that has weight and takes up space. The three states of matter are: **solid**, **liquid**, and **gas**. Some matter, like water, changes from one state to another when its temperature changes.

"Can *I* be in charge of the feeder this year?" I ask.

Abuelo smiles. "Yes, Javier. I think you are ready," he says. "Just remember to check it every day. Rufus is an early bird. He will need to get his food from us until the flowers bloom."

Liquids are wet and can be poured. They don't have their own shape. Instead, they take the shape of the container they are in—like the water inside the feeder.

The next day is very cold.
My neighbor Ana and I
can see our breath as we
play basketball.

Suddenly Rufus flies by! Ana gasps and
smiles. We stop our game to watch him.

Rufus lands on the feeder, but only for a
moment. Then he flies away.

"Why didn't he eat anything?" Ana asks me.

I take down the feeder and open the lid. The nectar looks kind of cloudy. I poke at it. *Tap, tap.* It's hard. "Ice!" I say.

Ana frowns. "You can't really sip ice."

Solids have their own fixed shape—though their shape can be changed by a force like stretching or squishing. Wood, fabric, and metal are solids. Water in its solid form is called ice.

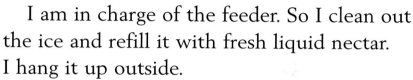

I am in charge of the feeder. So I clean out the ice and refill it with fresh liquid nectar. I hang it up outside.

A little while later, we see Rufus sipping from the feeder.

Ana gives me a high-five. Problem solved!

Freezing takes place when a liquid is cooled so much that it becomes a solid. Water freezes at a temperature of 32 degrees Fahrenheit.

But the next morning, there's more ice in the feeder. I take it inside.

When Abuelo wakes up, I show him the problem. "Look! There's ice—" I stop. The ice is gone. "There *was* ice in the feeder. Really!"

When a solid heats up enough to become a liquid, it's called **melting**. Solids like ice and candle wax melt easily. But even metals like gold can melt if they get hot enough!

"I believe it," Abuelo says. "It's been so cold overnight."

Poor Rufus, I think. He's the first hummingbird here. He's probably lonely. And on top of it, his food is too cold to eat. I imagine eating food straight out of the freezer. *Blech.*

I ask Abuelo to take me to the store after school. I want to see if I can find something to keep Rufus's nectar from freezing.

The store has heaters of all kinds. At first, nothing looks right for keeping nectar warm. I search every shelf. And then I find it!

"Look, Abuelo!" I say. "An outdoor water bowl for pets!" I read the package. The bowl plugs in. It keeps the water just warm enough so it won't freeze.

"¡Fantástico!" Abuelo says. "That's great. You can put Rufus's nectar in there."

Back at home, Ana is out in her yard. I call her over to show her the pet bowl. We plug it in and then fill the bowl with fresh nectar.
Will Rufus like it?

Ana and I play checkers while we wait.

Finally Rufus flies over. He zigs and zags over the new food bowl, checking it out. But then he darts away.

"Aww," I moan. "He didn't even try it!"

Then we see Rufus buzzing around Abuelo's bright-red sundial.

I have an idea! "The bowl is brown and boring," I point out. "But Abuelo says hummingbirds love red!"

I pour the nectar into Rufus's red feeder. I fill the pet bowl with plain water. Then I place the red feeder inside the bowl.

The next time we check, Rufus is at the feeder, having a snack. He likes it!

And our solution works. The next morning, the nectar is still liquid. The heater kept it from freezing overnight!

A **freezing point** is the temperature at which a liquid freezes. Mixing water with sugar lowers the water's freezing point. Sugar water turns to ice at around 26 degrees.

That afternoon, it's much warmer outside.
I check the feeder again. This time, it's almost
empty! "Wow! Rufus must be *super* hungry,"
I say to Ana.

Ana frowns. "Did he really drink all of that?
In one day?" She looks like she can't believe it.

We take the feeder inside to refill it. The tea kettle is whistling. Abuelo rushes in. "Whoops!" he says. "I left it boiling too long. Almost all my water is gone!"

"Gone?" I say. "Gone where?"

"Into the air," Abuelo explains. "When you heat water, it turns into steam. It evaporates."

Steam, or water vapor, is a **gas**. Gases are usually invisible. They spread out to fill the space they are in. When a liquid is heated enough to become a gas, it's called **evaporation**.

I look at Ana. Is she thinking what I'm thinking?

"Javier," she says, "during the day, it's warmer outside. Plus the extra heat from the pet bowl—"

"Makes the nectar evaporate!" I say. "Maybe we don't need the heater during the day."

The opposite of evaporation is **condensation**. That's when a gas is cooled enough to become a liquid. For example, when air touches a cold glass, you can often see droplets of condensation form on the glass.

Ana and I decide on a plan.

When it gets cold at night, I plug in the pet bowl. I unplug it in the morning when the temperature goes up.

I follow the plan for a couple of weeks. I check the feeder twice a day. I make sure there is always enough food for Rufus.

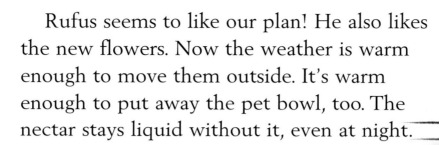

Rufus seems to like our plan! He also likes the new flowers. Now the weather is warm enough to move them outside. It's warm enough to put away the pet bowl, too. The nectar stays liquid without it, even at night.

It looks like spring has arrived.

But what about the other hummingbirds? Our regular birdfeeder is crowded with songbirds. But Rufus is still all alone.

I hear a whirr close by my ear. I turn. Rufus is drinking at the feeder. I've never been so close to a hummingbird before! I stand very still so I don't scare him away. Rufus stops to look up at me. He takes a few more sips.

Just then, I hear Ana whisper. "Javier!"
Slowly, I turn around.
There's another hummingbird! It is hovering over Ana's shoulder.

Rufus has some friends at last. I call for
Abuelo to come and see. Abuelo smiles at
all the hummingbirds whizzing around us.
"¡*Excelente!*" he says. "You know what we
have to do now, Javier?"

"I sure do," I tell him. "We have to make more nectar!"

THINK LIKE A SCIENTIST

Javier and Ana can do tests—and so can you! Scientists know that when their first try doesn't work, they have to make changes. They test out more options. Just like scientists, Javier and Ana tested ways to keep the nectar in a liquid state.

Look Back

- Re-read page 5. Why was the season important to this story?
- Look back at pages 22–24. What happened to the nectar? How did Javier and Ana figure this out?

Try This!

Make a Hummingbird Feeder
You will need: a red plastic cup, a hole punch, string, scissors, sugar, water, and measuring cups.

- Ask an adult to help you cut a hole in the shape of a half-circle halfway up the side of the cup.
- Use the hole punch to make two holes on opposite sides of the cup, near the top edge.
- Tie the string through the holes to create a loop.
- Mix 1/4 cup of sugar with 1 cup of water to make the nectar solution.
- Fill about the cup up to the hole.
- Hang the cup on a tree. Remember to keep it full and clean, and be patient!